SUITCASE

MILDRED PITTS WALTER

Illustrated by
TERESA FLAVIN

LOTHROP, LEE & SHEPARD BOOKS
New York

The text type is 14-point Stempel Schneidler.

Published by Lothrop, Lee & Shepard Books
a division of William Morrow and Company, Inc.
1350 Avenue of the Americas, New York, NY 10019
www.williammorrow.com

Printed in the United States of America.

3   5   7   9   10   8   6   4   2

LIBRARY OF CONGRESS CATALOGING-IN-PUBLICATION DATA
Walter, Mildred Pitts. Suitcase/by Mildred Pitts Walter;
illustrated by Teresa Flavin.
p. cm. Summary: Despite his love of drawing and his feelings of inadequacy as
an athlete, sixth-grader Xander "Suitcase" Bingham works to become a basketball
and baseball player to win the approval of his father.
ISBN 0-688-16547-8
[1. Self-perception—Fiction.   2. Fathers and sons—Fiction.   3. Artists—Fiction.
4. Afro-Americans—Fiction.]   I. Flavin, Teresa, ill.   II. Title.
PZ7.W17125Su 1999   [Fic]—DC21   99-11488   CIP

To Deborah Sims Fard

1

"Hey, Suitcase! Wait up," Ronnie called. The other boys with Ronnie laughed.

Xander didn't respond. He pretended he didn't know Ronnie was speaking to him, but he knew. Brandy, his sister, had taunted him with that same nickname at breakfast this morning.

"Hey, you hear me." Ronnie was not to be

ignored. "Are your suitcases so heavy you can't talk?" There was loud laughter.

Why couldn't they leave him alone? One nickname was enough. And as if he could read Xander's mind, Steve said, "He likes the name See-more better."

Xander's skin felt tight and tingly. He removed his backpack and held it close in front of him to help control the rage rising in his chest. He was so tense he thought he would break apart.

"You like See-more better?" Ronnie asked. "Man, your feet are bigger than you're tall. Because your feet so big, I'm gonna call you Suitcase."

Xander stopped. He glared at Ronnie and said in a low seething voice, "You better back off, man. I mean it, right now!"

"Hi, Alexander," Mrs. Cloud called.

Xander was relieved to hear the fine-arts teacher calling to him. His name was really Alexander. Only his family and friends called him Xander.

Mrs. Cloud continued, "I was hoping for someone nice. And here you are. Come, help me, please."

Xander did not respond to her happy greeting as she loaded him down with books and papers.

"Is something wrong?" Mrs. Cloud asked.

"No, ma'am." He spoke just loud enough for her to hear. He said nothing more as he walked behind her to her room.

"There *is* something wrong," Mrs. Cloud said when Xander had deposited the things on her desk and was standing with his head down. He looked up. She smiled and said, "You can tell me."

Xander remembered the conversation between his mama and daddy that had also taken place that morning.

"Why can't he be like his sister?" Daddy had asked. "We never have to wake her up. And when she was eleven she was interested and active in a lotta things. I don't know what's wrong with that boy. He's interested in nothing but fooling around with that drawing."

"I see nothing wrong with drawing if that's what he wants to do," Mama said. "And he's good at it."

"It's not likely he'll make a living out of drawing. And artists don't get college scholarships as easily as ballplayers. He needs to mix with boys and men more, not sit in that room drawing all the time."

Still feeling the hurt from his daddy's words, Xander couldn't bring himself to confide in Mrs. Cloud. He said with a tinge of agitation, "It's nothing." Yet he was grateful when Mrs. Cloud asked him to stay and help her change her bulletin board. And he was glad that she didn't make him talk while they worked. He measured the bulletin board and placed borders for students' paintings.

As he gathered his things to leave, she said, "You know you're still my favorite artist, don't you?"

Xander did not know what to say. He just stood with his head down.

"Don't you?" she asked.

"Yes, ma'am." He looked at her and smiled.

He remembered being voted best artist in

the whole school last year when he was in the fifth grade. Ronnie, who had entered the competition, too, had said after the ceremony, "You don't draw that good, you just so tall you see more than the rest of us." Now, he could still hear the laughter from his classmates.

"Doing much drawing these days?" Mrs. Cloud asked.

"Right now I'm trying to draw animals," Xander said softly.

"You're very good with people. I wish more of my students had your eye, Alexander," she said. "Thank you for doing the bulletin board, it looks great."

He rushed out of her room not minding at all that he was six feet two inches tall, wearing a size thirteen shoe.

2

That good feeling did not last long. Xander's first class was in the gym. In that large lofty room he should have moved with ease, but there he felt awkward, unable to control his body and make it do what he wanted it to do.

"Bingham," Mr. Sterling called as Xander entered the gym. The coach called all the boys by their last names. "No excuses today, and I want you dressed on time."

The rest of the class was already in the locker room. Xander moved slowly. He knew what was coming, and the minute he stepped out of his pants, it started. "Ohoo, look at those stilt-stick legs," a voice said.

"And chopstick thighs," said another.

"Man, you'd think he could run with all them legs, eh?" said Ronnie.

"Uh-uh, him? He's more on his face than his feet," Steve said.

Luckily his taunters, who loved basketball, rushed out to the floor. When Xander finally got on the court, the class was warming up. Most of the boys loved the game. Gym rats. When they were not at school, they spent much of their time shooting hoop.

Ronnie and a boy named Craig were chosen hoop captains for the day. Xander waited— maybe Craig would choose him. He waited. Last man.

"All right, Sims, Bingham will go on your team." Sims was Ronnie's last name.

"No way, Coach, naw. Put him in his best

position, benchwarmer." All the boys howled with laughter.

"Enough of your antics, Sims."

The familiar feeling of shame and hurt rose up into Xander's throat. Even though he hated being called a benchwarmer, he came back with, "I don't mind sitting out, Coach. Let me keep time and scores."

"No way. I'm on to you, Bingham. You are up today. With Sims."

Xander's heart pounded, and his knees felt like jelly. He moved awkwardly up and down the court and under the basket, but nobody passed him the ball. Finally, the ball came toward him. It went right through his fingers. Ball outside.

It was Xander's ball to return to play. He was nervous and excited as he stood looking for an open teammate. He threw, but the ball landed in the hands of an opposing player. His team-mates howled.

"Stupid!" Ronnie shouted.

Xander, more determined than ever, tried to

retrieve the ball. He stayed close to the man, hoping to block the shot. But he moved in too close. Being so tall and awkward he could not back off quickly enough and over-guarded. Foul. The free thrower scored. Ronnie called for time-out. "Listen, See-more—"

"My name is not See-more. You call me Xander."

"Listen, whatever, you can't play, man. You got nothing but weak moves, so don't be pretending you can play some hoop."

Xander came right back. "You're not calling the shots here. Coach is. I'm in the game."

Ronnie broke huddle, and the game resumed.

Within minutes Xander was fouled. He missed the free throw. His team groaned, to the opponents' glee. Xander's face clouded over with disappointment. Before he could make any more errors, the bell rang.

3

Xander zipped his jacket against the cold winter wind as he left school in a hurry. He was anxious to get back to the drawing he had started the night before. When he arrived home, the warmth and aroma of good things cooking greeted him. "What's up, Ma?" he called.

His mama was on the phone. "He's coming in right now," Xander heard her say. "So they've asked you to help with the basketball team at the center. That's nice, Aaron." Then she turned to Xander. "Here, your daddy wants to talk to you."

"Hi, what's happening?" As Xander listened, he frowned. "Do I have to go? Naw. I don't want to. Can't we talk about it when you get home?" He hung up the phone. "Aw, man! He won't even discuss it."

"Why you upset? You should be happy you're going to the center with your daddy tonight. We're having an early dinner so you two can be out of here around six."

"I don't want to play basketball at the center. Do I have to go, Mama?"

"That's what your daddy said. He's been wanting you to play basketball for a long time. Now he's willing to work with a team. I bet he's doing it just to get you involved."

"I don't want to play basketball." He remembered not even ringing the hoop with the free throw in gym class. "It would be fun if I could play. But I can't."

"No such thing as can't, Xander. You can learn anything if you want to."

"Ma, it's nothing to do with wanting to. I can't, and I'm not going."

"Now, you know your daddy is set on your playing with him. He thinks you're lazy and don't want to ruin your long, slender artist's fingers." She laughed.

"It's not funny. You don't know how hard I try. I just can't play." Frustrated and angry, Xander went to his room. He sat on the floor with his back against his bed, his long legs stretched out before him. The excitement he had felt about drawing had disappeared. He felt a lump in his throat that might at any minute turn into tears. But he told himself he must not cry. It wasn't worth it.

He got up and looked at the drawing he had done the night before. He was not pleased with the tiger's paws. They were the hardest things for him to do. He began to erase and redraw, and the joy of drawing took over. Just as he was beginning to feel that what he was drawing looked like tiger paws, not feet, Brandy yelled from the foot of the stairs.

"Hey, See-more! Dad's home. Dinner's ready."

Xander stormed out of his room and raced down the stairs. "You had better stop calling me names." He glowered down at Brandy. "I don't want to hurt you."

"What's the matter, Xander? You're so cranky today," his mama said.

"My name is not See-more. Tell her to stop calling me that."

"Okay, you two, sit down. After we eat, I want to know what this is about," their daddy said.

Xander sighed, wishing he could leave the table. But he was always too hungry to go without a meal.

"Daddy, basketball schedule is out today," Brandy said. "Our first game is next week. I know we'll win that game 'cause our opponents are really no basketball material. I expect you to come."

"I don't care much for those one-sided games. But I always come. Wouldn't miss seeing my girl, you know that. Anything exciting with you, Xander?"

"Not much—"

"You know Mr. Hamilton, our English teacher?" Brandy interrupted. "He started a Dunbar writing club. He asked me to join."

Why couldn't she give him time, Xander thought. She always had so much to tell about herself.

"Dunbar for Paul Lawrence, the poet?" Mama asked.

"You got it."

"I hope you said yes."

"You know I did."

Mama turned to Xander. "You sure you have nothing to tell?"

"Yeah, like how'd you do in gym class today?" Brandy snickered.

"I think Xander can speak for himself," Daddy said.

"I said, nothing." Xander kept his eyes on his plate and finished eating.

"Aw, come on, tell us, See-more," Brandy said.

"Brandy, I don't like your attitude. Stop being so smart-alecky with him," Mama said.

"And what is this See-more business?"

"The kids call him that because he's so tall," Brandy said.

"Xander can do absolutely nothing about his size," Daddy said.

"Xander got his tall genes from my side of the family," Mama said. "You don't go around here making fun of your grandpa and your uncles. You think they're handsome."

"They are handsome. So? What's that got to do with Xander?"

"A lot," Mama said. "Just give him time."

"Aw, it's just fun, Mama."

"It is not fun for me," Xander said.

"It's not fun, period. So don't ever use those words to him again." Daddy was firm. "You hear me?"

"I hear you," Brandy muttered with a sullen look.

Xander returned her look with a grin.

4

Why doesn't he slow down, Xander thought as he walked to the center with his daddy. He struggled to keep control of his legs and feet, thinking that any moment he might fall on his face and embarrass himself.

There were twelve boys already at the center when Xander and his daddy arrived. Enough for a good team. Ronnie and Steve, the gym rats, were there, anxious to show what great players

they were. They *should* be good, Xander thought. When they weren't sleeping or eating, they were hooping.

While they were waiting for the main coach, there was a shoot-around. Balls shot from every angle on the court were falling into and around the net. Xander watched his daddy dribble the ball down the court, switching from his left hand to his right. Shooting from the middle of the court, he hit nothing but net.

"A smooth, lean, mean machine, with a cool crossover, man," Ronnie said.

Xander looked at his daddy. Six feet, long-legged and long-armed, with hardly any fat on his body, he moved with ease. Xander appreciated his daddy's move, too. But with an artist's eye. The body is beautiful playing basketball, he thought. All parts working together, like music. If only he could draw that. His daddy tried a layup and missed. He caught the rebound and slammed it through the hoop.

"I'm looking at you. Man, you should be in

the NBA," Jeff, the director and coach of the center, said as he came on the floor.

ᐟ Xander's daddy laughed. "Missed my chance. Too old for that now. I'm gonna leave it to my offspring here. This is my son, Alexander; Alexander, Jeff. We all call him Xander."

Jeff, about a half-inch taller than Xander, won Xander's respect right away when he asked, "What's your sport, man?" He didn't assume that Xander was a basketball player like most people did.

Xander heard snickering. His scalp tingled, and he lowered his head. "I don't have a sport," he said. Then sensing that his daddy was not pleased with his answer, he added, "Not yet."

"We'll make a good center out of him," his daddy said. "He's tall enough."

"Yeah, I'll find a game for him," Jeff said. Ronnie and Steve smirked.

Jeff blew his whistle. "Let's get to work here now. I want to see what you guys can do. Form a big circle. We're gonna get accustomed to the feel of the ball. I want you to become good at throwing and catching chest passes. Show me now how you handle the ball."

Steve stood next to Xander, and Ronnie placed himself across from them. Xander had the urge to move, but he wouldn't give them the satisfaction of knowing that they intimidated him. Ronnie's passes were fast and hard, from the chest and from overhead. Xander caught most of them but couldn't get the ball off his chest fast enough.

"Pay attention, Xander. Concentrate," his daddy shouted at him.

The ball was bounced from one player to another, around the circle. Xander's hands and fingers did not fail him. And the longer they practiced, the better he did.

"Attention, men," Jeff shouted. "You did good. Now I want to see you do your stuff, running, passing, and tossing for the hoop. You run, I pass you the ball, you go for the net. Okay?"

It looked easy, but Xander could not catch and hold the ball. His palms were wet with sweat; his knees and legs were rubbery. He tripped over his feet and fell.

Ronnie passed by Xander and muttered, "Turnover king."

"Time-out," Jeff called. Xander sat on the floor, head down on his arms, arms folded on his drawn-up knees. He dared not look at his daddy. He felt too ashamed. When Jeff called for them to line up for running and tossing at the basket again, Xander walked over and sat on the bench. He would rather be called a benchwarmer than a turnover king for losing the ball to the opponent.

Xander and his daddy walked home with Jeff and some of the other boys. Most of the boys knew his daddy because he worked in the biggest sports store downtown. They all laughed and joked. All except Xander.

"You do some good slamming, Mr. Bingham," Steve said.

"I like your handles better. You dribble all over the place and nobody can touch you," Ronnie said. "I can learn some stuff from you, Mr. Bingham."

When they went their separate ways, Jeff said, "I'll see you next time, Xander." Xander didn't answer. As the boys walked on, Ronnie, thinking he was out of earshot, said, "Man, if I had a daddy like that, I could play up some hoops."

"Well, how did it go, Xander?" Mama asked when they walked into the house.

"All right," Xander said without enthusiasm. "I guess."

"There're kids out there who give their all. Xander didn't try hard enough tonight, but he'll get better," his daddy said.

Xander sighed.

"Got cookies and milk," Mama said.

Without looking at her he said, "No, thanks," and went straight to his room.

He sat in the dark, thinking. How could his daddy say he hadn't tried hard enough? Angry, he undressed and lay on his bed. *What does he know? I try, but I can't please him. I'll never play like him. He plays better'n anybody around here, and he knows it.*

He lay thinking about his daddy's smooth moves. Suddenly Xander was excited about bringing alive on paper what he had seen in the gym. He jumped out of bed and hurriedly took out his drawing pencils. What would he try to capture? His daddy's hop-jump to the hoop? His dribbling? He decided on the hop-jump.

Xander closed his eyes and tried to see what he had seen when his daddy was playing. The body and ball moving with rhythm, and the weightlessness as the body hung in air. He started in with strong lines, then used quick, upward strokes, moving from dark to light lines as he sketched the body.

When it was done, the body looked fine, but the open hand ready to release the ball was not as he had seen it. He drew and erased that hand again and again. Finally, he gave up. Looking at his work, overall, he was pleased.

Back in bed, he tried to hang on to the good feeling he had about his drawing, but his mind went back to the center and to his daddy's words that he hadn't tried hard enough. He saw himself in that circle, then sprawled on the floor, and again he felt the sting of shame. Why? If only his daddy knew how hard he tried. If only he could accept the fact that Xander couldn't play basketball.

Did Jeff understand, he wondered? Jeff hadn't assumed that he could play basketball just because he was tall. Xander felt that Jeff was not like the others.

Was there some game he could be good at? Maybe. Could Jeff become a friend? Maybe. But more than anything he wanted his daddy to be proud of him.

Yet all he saw in his daddy's eyes was disappointment. Xander fell into troubled sleep.

5

Xander walked from school through the park. He passed the flying rings, the hand-over-hand ladder, and the trapeze. None of these interested him. He made his way to a wire stretched close to the ground. This wire was used to increase balance skills. Xander called it "the steady tester."

As he came closer to the wire he was surprised to see Jeff there with a group of men.

Xander moved to watch as, one at a time, the men tried to walk across the wire. He stood in awe, even though their arms flailed and they fell off almost immediately. As many times as he had tried, he had never even been able to get on the wire.

Then Jeff got on. For a long time, he stood still on the end of the wire to balance himself. It was so quiet that only the hum of the distant city could be heard. Then Jeff moved slowly but with assurance, until he reached the other end of the wire.

Everybody applauded. Xander was so excited that he ran to Jeff and said, "Way to go, man."

"Thanks, Xander. You take a turn."

"Not me. No, no, no."

Xander was glad that Jeff did not insist that he walk the wire.

"Last night you said you had no game," Jeff said. "What do you like best? Baseball? Basketball? Football?"

"I guess I like them all. I just can't play."

"But which do you like best?"

"Aw, I don't know." He thought of telling Jeff that the only thing he really liked was working with pencils and paints. What will Jeff think if I tell him that? He might not like me, Xander thought. He decided to keep that his secret.

"You know what? If you really want to learn a game, I can help you. You know what you need?"

"Naw."

"You just need to make your body do what you want it to do. And you need to want to do that so bad, man, that you'll do whatever it takes to make your body do it. I can give you the tools. How you use them is up to you. If you really want to, you will."

"I try, but I fall all over the place."

"Xander, do you jump rope?"

Xander giggled. "What? Girls jump rope."

"Great athletes jump rope," Jeff said. "Jump rope, and then I'll teach you to walk that wire."

Xander was not sure about jumping rope,

but he just knew he'd do almost anything to learn to walk that wire the way Jeff did. "I don't know," he mumbled. "Maybe. I'll try."

"You'll like jumping rope, what you bet. Wait right here. I'll get a rope." Jeff returned and said, "Watch me." He grasped the rope and started to jump. His tall, lean body seemed to float as the rope whirred. His arms and hands crisscrossed swiftly. Xander wondered if he could learn to jump rope like that!

When he tried, his feet got entangled and his arms and hands bumped into each other. He was so frustrated, he was ready to give up.

"Takes practice, man, lots of practice," Jeff said again and again.

"Why do I have to jump rope to learn to walk the wire?"

"Jumping rope will help you develop balance. You won't walk that wire without great balance. And until all of your body can work together, hands, eyes, and feet, man, you won't catch or hit a ball. There are three things: jumping rope, walking that wire, and practicing a game. Put them all together and you can make a fine ballplayer. That would make your papa proud."

Jeff gave him a rope so that he could practice at home. But Xander still was not sure he wanted to do it. And he certainly didn't want Ronnie and Steve and his daddy seeing him with a jump rope in his hands. Where at home could he jump? He couldn't practice in his room. They all would hear him and know. And when could he do it out of sight? It would have to be done late at night, out behind the garage.

Every night Xander slipped out of his room and jumped rope, trying to get his legs and feet to obey and his arms and hands to move smoothly and swiftly. In a couple of weeks his feet did begin to obey; he jumped faster and faster. If only he could get his arms and hands under control. He practiced and practiced. Then one night he had just gotten back to his room when he heard footsteps heading toward his door. Xander jumped into bed with all his clothes on. The light was still on.

He lay still with the cover up around his ears wishing he was in the dark. His daddy opened the door and said, "That boy, sleeping with the light on."

Afraid his thumping heart could be heard, Xander dared not breathe. His daddy turned off the light and closed the door. Whew! Xander thought. He lay there, afraid to move, and fell asleep with all his clothes on.

After that he spent more time at the center jumping. For weeks he and Jeff also worked with the basketball, tossing it overhead and from the chest. "You're getting better," Jeff said. "That ball is coming harder and faster."

Xander didn't think he was getting better. But every day he worked harder. Now Jeff also had him do line drills—running up and down the court to improve his skills. There was only one thing Xander really liked—the mask drill. With his back to Jeff, Xander would turn quickly and catch the ball when Jeff threw it to him. Jeff was surprised at how well Xander did. He never missed. "Man, you know, you good at this."

Jeff also showed him how to stand flat-footed on the paint near the basket. When the ball was passed to Xander, all he had to do was turn, hop, and put the ball through the net. Xander soon learned that his height was an advantage. He could easily rebound and keep an opponent from scoring.

Soon he was not only able to stand at the free-throw line, hit the backboard, and rim the ball into the basket—sometimes he was able to score hitting nothing but net.

The first time he hit nothing but net, Jeff shouted, "Great!" and hugged him. Xander was so happy he couldn't say or do anything. He just let himself be hugged.

Even though he had improved, nobody seemed to notice except Jeff. But one day Coach Sterling for the first time, without warning, announced, "Bingham, you're hoop captain today."

"Oh naaaw!" rang out from the class.

"Yes, Bingham. Choose a team."

Xander couldn't believe it. Why was Coach

doing this to him? Baffled, he went forward to call men for his team. Each man he chose came unwillingly, with a frown on his face. Still, Xander was determined to show them what he had learned. He placed himself in position to score, he waved, he called, but the ball never came his way. Angry and frustrated, he wanted to do the unforgivable thing—walk off the court to leave his team on their own.

6

Weeks went by. Now Xander jumped rope so fast and lightly that he seemed to float. His hands and feet obeyed his commands. One day at the center he was jumping, enjoying himself, and didn't notice Ronnie and his friends in the room until Ronnie shouted, "Look at him. So. Coach found your sport!"

"Yeah, he can get his feet up for a jump rope but not for a jump shot," one of the boys said.

"Hey, there's a girls' double-Dutch competition going on right now in the park, and there's a skirt waiting, just your size," Ronnie said.

Xander wanted the floor to open and swallow him up. His scalp tingled, his face burned with anger. Suddenly he moved to get Ronnie, but Ronnie, quick as a flash, ran away laughing. There was so much loud laughter, Jeff came into the room. "Okay, okay, fellows, chill out," Jeff shouted.

"Coach, he's in here jumping rope like a girl," Steve said, pointing toward Xander. They couldn't stop laughing.

"I thought you guys were smarter than that. Anybody who wants to be strong and steady jumps rope."

"They ignorant and think they so smart," Xander said. "Coach, why don't you show them how to really jump rope?"

Jeff got a rope and began jumping. He moved his arms, hands, and feet very fast. Xander jumped with him. In perfect rhythm, their ropes made one whirring sound.

"That's the real deal man," Ronnie said.

"It's good, all good. That's a man's way of jumping rope," Steve said. "Show us how to do it, Coach." They all clamored to learn how to jump rope.

Later, at dinner, Xander ate slowly to delay the time when he would have to tell what happened that day. Brandy had her say. He sat looking down at his plate.

"Okay, son, your turn," Daddy said.

Xander's chest tightened, and he could feel his hands beginning to sweat. "Oh, nothing much." Then he blurted out, "Today I was jumping rope at the center—"

Brandy interrupted with a scream, "Jumping rope! Lord, that's all I need. A brother who is an artist and a rope jumper."

"Stop it, Brandy," Mama said. "Let him finish. What happened?"

Now Xander was not so sure he should tell. "Go on, Xander," Daddy said.

"These guys saw me jumping rope and laughed at me—"

"See? See?" Brandy said. "Girls jump rope. Why does he always have to do stupid things?"

"That's exactly what they said, 'Girls jump rope,'" Xander went on. He told how Jeff and he had jumped together in perfect rhythm. "After they saw us, all the guys wanted to learn to jump like that."

"Why didn't I think of jumping rope for you, Xander?" Daddy said. "It's the best thing for building balance and stamina. Brandy, I thought you knew. The best boxers always get in shape by jumping rope."

Xander's chest expanded with pride. "She don't know a thing. And thinks she knows so much," he said.

"I know more'n you," Brandy shot back.

"That's enough now," Mama said.

"You always siding with Xander." She jumped up from the table and ran to her room.

Mama followed, and Xander could hear their raised voices. "I don't like the way you're acting toward your brother."

"You don't know," Brandy wailed. "He looks

funny, and when people laugh at him, it hurts. He shouldn't be doing silly things to make it worse. What he does affects me, too."

His mama's voice was too low for Xander to hear what the question was. But Brandy screamed out her answer, "Yes, yes, I'm ashamed of him. He's always embarrassing me."

Xander thought his chest would explode and his head would leave his body. Brandy ignored him at school, but he just thought it was because she was in the upper building. He didn't know she felt that way.

He couldn't hear how his mother responded before coming back to the table. In complete silence she reached over and covered Xander's hand with hers. Finally, Daddy suggested, "Why don't you go and get your jump rope and show us what you can do." Xander was reluctant.

"Aw, come on. Don't be shy, Xander. Go on, get your rope," Mama pleaded.

"Okay, come outside and I'll show you," Xander said. At first he jumped slowly and did some easy footwork. Then he moved faster,

then faster until he felt like he was floating, his feet hardly touching the ground.

For a few minutes he was even able to criss-cross his arms.

"Wow! Xander, that's just great." Mama beamed.

"Let me take a stab at it." His daddy took the rope. He tripped up a couple of times at the beginning. But when he got going, he did some fancy footwork and crisscrossed his hands and arms easily.

"Aaron!" Mama said. "Pretty good for an old man."

"You never told us you jump rope, Daddy," Xander said excitedly.

"You never asked me."

Back in his room, Xander was glad that his father had asked him to jump rope for them, but he was still stung by what Brandy had said. He remembered when he was only seven and as tall as boys in the fourth grade. A boy pushed him around and called him a second-grade retard. Brandy stood toe-to-toe with the bully and told him, "This is my little brother. He's no retard. You mess with him, you mess with me." Now she had joined them with her teasing.

He wanted to forget her and stop the pain. He took out his animal drawing. Something still was not right with his tiger's paws. He drew and erased, drew and erased, but he just couldn't make them look the way he thought paws should look. Was all that attention to jumping rope and trying to shoot hoops making him lose his touch? He wondered.

He put the tiger away and sat doodling, thinking about what had happened at the dinner table. Before he knew it, he was sketching his daddy jumping rope.

There was a knock on his door. It was Brandy. "I'm sorry about what I said. But you don't know. It hurts me when they hurt you."

"I don't know? It's *me* they laughing at. But it's okay. I understand." There was silence between them.

She looked over his shoulders at the sketch

and said, "Hey, that's Daddy jumping rope. Pretty good. Pretty good."

"You like it?"

"Yeah. And you're a good jumper, too."

"How do you know? You didn't see me."

"Oh, but I did. I was looking out of my window." She put her hands on his shoulders and kissed the top of his head. "I love you, but you do get on my nerves. Good night."

Xander lay in bed feeling better than he had felt in a long time. He was happy to know that Brandy was still in his corner and that his daddy was pleased about him jumping rope. Brandy was right, the sketch of his daddy jumping rope was pretty good.

Even though he had not drawn the tiger's paw as well as he wanted, he knew that sooner or later he would. But he was not so sure about walking that wire. Maybe that too would come. He smiled and curled up in the covers. That night he slept without dreaming.

The next morning he was up early. For the

first time, he was in the bathroom before Brandy and was at the breakfast table on time. He ate as much as he wanted.

Brandy said to him, "You eat enough to feed a horse."

Xander was about to respond when Daddy said, "He's a big boy and still growing. Son, why didn't you tell me you were jumping rope?"

Xander beamed and said, "You didn't ask me."

7

Each day Xander got better and better with the jump rope and the basketball handling. Still, none of the team captains wanted him to play on their teams. And when playing at the center under the critical eye of his father, he didn't do well at all.

"You're good, man," Jeff often said to him. "I can tell you that all day, but if you don't believe it, you won't be good. Where is your self-confidence?"

"You say I'm good because you like me. And you're the only one. Nobody likes me."

"Why you say that?"

Xander lowered his head. "Because it's true. I hate school. Kids laugh at me." He stopped, wondering if he should tell Jeff what was really happening. Jeff waited. "Yeah," Xander went on. "They call me See-more and Suitcase because I'm tall, with big feet." He still could not look at Jeff. "And I'll tell you something else. I hate basketball."

"Oh, Xander. People tease thinking it's fun, not knowing how they really hurt. Do you know why your feet are so big? You're gonna grow up and fill out to be a big man. You might even get taller."

Xander still did not look up as Jeff went on. "You *need* big feet. Suppose you had feet like the others who are now laughing at you. You'd be walking around here like this." Jeff hobbled across the room as if he could hardly stand up.

Xander laughed. "You really think I'll grow bigger and grow into my feet?"

"Yes! You're already almost as tall as I am. Believe me. And then those people who are calling you See-more and Suitcase will be looking up to you. Literally!" He laughed.

Xander didn't laugh because it was hard to believe he would ever control his body. As if Jeff knew what he was thinking, he said, "Now you listen to me. I say you're good because I know where you were when you started. You could hardly hold the ball. Now you are hop-jumping, dribbling, and making baskets from the free-throw line. You'll have to get out there and show them what you can do. And what's this hating the hoop game?"

"I just don't like it. I'll never be good at it."

"It's up to you."

"What I'd really like is to walk that wire," Xander said.

"Your rope jumping is so good I think you might be ready for the wire."

"You think so? Really?"

"Don't get too excited, now. Walking that wire is much harder than jumping rope."

The first time Xander tried the wire, he could not stay on for even one second. "My feet too big," he cried.

"No such thing as your feet being too big."

"Why can't I stay on?"

"Xander. It won't happen the first time you get your feet on the wire. Don't be so impatient."

The days grew warmer and longer. Xander spent as much time as he could at the park practicing on the wire. Soon he was able to stand for a few seconds with both feet on the end of the wire.

Ronnie and his friends were often in the park too, on the hand-over-hand bars and the trapeze. One day after school, Xander was concentrating on balancing at the end of the wire when Ronnie and some of Ronnie's friends walked nearby.

"Hey, look who's on the wire. Suitcase himself," Ronnie shouted, and they all ran over.

"What you trying to do? Bend the wire with your big feet?"

Xander surprised himself when he calmly said, "No, I'm here to walk it." He stood still, concentrating, balancing, and then for the very first time he moved one foot ahead of the other. But when he was about to make the second step, his arms flailed and he fell off.

"Is that the best you can do?" Ronnie jeered.

"That's better'n you can do," Craig said, and all the boys laughed.

"I can do that good, what you bet?" answered Ronnie.

"Show us, show us," they all cried.

"I don't have to show you nothing." Huffed, Ronnie walked away.

"How long you been working on the wire, man?" asked Steve.

"Long enough," Xander answered coolly and quickly.

"Just think, man, when you do get going you'll walk it pretty quick 'cause your feet are so long," Craig said. Xander joined in the laughter.

They all took turns, and no one could get both feet on the wire. And I thought I was so out of control, Xander said to himself, feeling better than he had in a long time. His confidence improved and so did his game skills.

One day when he was the last man chosen on Steve's team, playing opposite Ronnie, Xander placed himself flat-footed on the paint under the net. Every time Ronnie went for the basket, Xander blocked the shot and kept him from scoring.

"Way to go, Bingham," Coach shouted. "Stick to him."

Xander scooped and dunked every rebound he made. But his team did not win. However, in the end Coach reported, "Today the top scorer on Steve Parker's team is none other than Alexander Bingham." The team clapped and Xander's chest expanded.

8

"You're a very dependable young man, Xander," said Jeff as Xander entered the center. "How would you like to become an assistant?"

"Me?"

"Yeah, you."

From that day on Xander helped with games, keeping time, keeping scores, and refereeing midget basketball. Jeff also let him work with the smaller kids, who always got excited when Xander gave them attention. Sometimes he showed them tricks with folded paper, and sometimes he told them stories as he drew circles, triangles, and squares.

His happiest time at the center was when he helped out in the art room. All the kids gathered around him and insisted that he make things for them, or help them with the things they were making.

One day the space was almost empty, so Xander sat drawing alone. He was busy making quick strokes on a strong curved scoop, sketching a tall lean figure dribbling a basketball. Jeff was surprised.

"Un-huh! That's pretty good," Jeff said. "Seeing you draw like that, now I know why you're so good at the mask drill. I bet you'd be good at baseball."

"What's drawing good got to do with baseball?"

"Well, you have to have good eye-hand coordination to draw and to hit a ball. You know, you just *might* be good at baseball."

"Aw, I don't know."

"Well, we can soon find out. Want to try?"

Jeff rounded up the kids in the center to go outside and field some balls. Xander stepped up to the plate to try to hit Jeff's pitches. He was amazed. If he waited until the ball was almost upon him to swing the bat, he could hit the ball easily and with a lot of power.

Jeff too was surprised and pleased. "You can hit, now let's see if you can pitch," he said.

Xander threw the ball and no matter how hard Jeff tried, he could not hit it. Xander grinned.

Jeff grinned back. "You're very good. You ever heard of Satchel Paige?"

"What kinda name is that, Satchel?" Xander laughed.

"He was a great pitcher. Got the name Satchel because he had big feet. Ring a bell?"

"I guess a satchel is a kind of suitcase, right?" Xander asked and grinned.

"Yeah, right. And Satchel Paige was among the

greatest. Maybe you'll be too, one day. Wait'll your daddy see how you can throw a ball."

"He won't care," Xander said just above a whisper.

"Why you say your daddy won't care?"

"I just know." He lowered his head.

"I bet your daddy cares about the things you do, especially if you do them well."

Xander remembered what his daddy had said about his drawing. Maybe his daddy would be proud of him if he played baseball. I could like baseball, he thought, but I love drawing. "No, he won't care."

"How do you know?" Jeff asked.

"He never talks to me like he talks to other people. I don't think he loves me."

"You know, some people can talk and say 'I love you,' easily. But they're never there when you need them. They don't do anything for you. Saying they love you is enough for them. But your daddy is always there for you, man. That's love."

Xander did not know what to say. He wanted to believe Jeff. He remembered Brandy and the jump-rope scene. His daddy had defended him then. And when he saw him jump rope, his daddy praised him. Jeff was right, maybe.

9

Spring arrived. The days warmed, the grass turned green, and buds on trees burst forth as leaves. The gym class moved outdoors to the baseball field. Although Xander felt a little more comfortable playing baseball, he was never given the chance to really play.

As in basketball, he was chosen at the end of the lineup. He always played outfield and seldom had a chance to come to the plate to bat. Baseball was not the in thing, anyway; Craig was the only one who was excited about the game. Everybody else was into hooping. And Xander was into drawing.

"I'm looking for sixth graders for the school team," Coach said one day at gym practice. "Good pitchers are what I need. Everybody is going to have a chance to show me what he can do." Coach walked to the batting plate.

Xander's palms began to sweat. He knew he could throw and hit the ball with Jeff, but he didn't know if he could make the ball do what he wanted it to do in front of the coach and his class. Nervously he waited his turn.

Finally Coach called, "Bingham, come on, throw me a ball."

Xander walked slowly to the mound. He could hardly breathe, he was so uptight. When the catcher threw the ball, it went right through Xander's hands. He chased it down, trying to ignore the laughter. On the mound he said to

himself, Calm down and concentrate. Look at the catcher's mitt. He stood still and took a deep breath. He threw the ball.

The ball went straight, then just as the coach struck at it, the ball dipped slightly. Strike! Xander took his time. Again he took a deep breath, looked at the catcher's mitt, and fired the ball. The ball curved slightly out. Strike!

Xander sensed the quiet and the eyes of the class on him. Again he took his time. He concentrated on the mitt and pitched. Coach swung. The ball went slightly up. Coach struck out and walked over to the mound.

"Bingham, who taught you to pitch like that?"

"Nobody."

"You can tell me. Somebody had to."

"Nobody."

"With some training you'll be an asset to us. I'm going to give you a chance on the team."

Xander couldn't believe this was happening to him. "Me? You mean it? I can play for the Mustangs?"

"If you want that chance, I mean it, Bingham."

Xander trembled with excitement. Could he do it? He blurted out, "Yeah, Coach, yeah, I wanna try."

The rest of the day all the boys were talking about Xander and how he struck out the coach with a dip ball, and how maybe he'd play on the school team.

"How do you make the ball do that?" Craig wanted to know.

"I just throw it, that's all."

"It's more'n that," Steve said. "Tell us, man, how you do it?"

"I don't know. I've always liked throwing things, trying to make them do funny stuff. I guess I'm good at it 'cause I do it so much."

On the way home from school Ronnie and Steve dominated the conversation, still talking about how sorry they were that the basketball season was over. When they entered the park,

Steve said, "Let's go by the steady tester. I bet I can last longer than anybody."

"Not longer than me," Ronnie said.

"You been practicing?" asked Xander.

"I don't have to practice. I'm just good like that."

Xander stifled a laugh. He knew walking that wire took lots of practice.

"Who'll go first?" Steve asked.

"Let's toss," Ronnie said. "Heads me; tails, you, Steve. Xander, you last."

Steve went first. He had a hard time standing on the end of the wire to start. Finally, he balanced and started across. Two steps and he lost control. Down he came. Ronnie balanced on the wire quicker, but he had not gone much farther than Steve before his arms flailed and he came down.

Xander watched them nervously. Would he be able to walk as well as he had been doing recently? He stepped on and fastened his eyes on the wire and stood still for a long time. Nobody made a sound. Then he slid one foot on the wire. He took another step, then another. Halfway across, his arms flailed, but he balanced himself and moved on. Slowly, slowly, and just near the end, he lost control and stepped off.

"Wow!" the boys cried.

"And with your big feet," Ronnie said.

"Yeah, big feet and all, I did it," Xander said and laughed.

When Xander went his way, all the boys said, "See you, man." All except Ronnie. He said, "See you, See-more."

Xander, suddenly knowing he could live with that name said, "Not if I see you first."

That evening at dinner he didn't wait to be asked what had happened to him that day. He proudly said, "I struck out the coach, and he said he'd give me a chance with the Mustangs if I wanted to. I could be a pitcher."

"And what was your answer?" asked Daddy.

"I said yeah."

"Wow, Xander," Mama said.

"Great way to go, son," Daddy said.

Xander could hardly contain his excitement. "And you know what? I walked farther than anybody on the low tightwire today."

Brandy was speechless. Xander would have liked for his daddy to hug him the way Jeff had when he made his first basket hitting nothing but net. But his daddy was not the hugging kind. Xander was happy just knowing his daddy was pleased.

10

Everyone was sitting in class, waiting for the bell to end the day, when a voice came over the loudspeaker, "Alexander Bingham, please go to Mrs. Cloud's room."

"What you gonna do, Suitcase, play with the paints?"

"Aw, Ronnie, you're so crude," one of the girls said.

"Yeah, man, lay off," Steve said.

Xander dismissed Ronnie with a wave of his hand and rushed to Mrs. Cloud's room.

"I have some good news, Alexander. There is a district-wide contest for a banner to be used at the City Spirit Art Festival. Our school has been invited to participate. We want *you* to do our banner."

"Who, me?" Xander asked, surprised.

His daddy's voice echoed in his mind. *"I don't know what's wrong with that boy. He's interested in nothing but fooling around with that drawing. He needs to mix with boys and men more, not sit in that room drawing all the time."*

"Oh, no. No, ma'am. I can't."

"What do you mean, you can't?"

He sighed deeply. "I don't know. Do I have to tell you right now? Let me think about it."

"Oh, Alexander, I know you can do it. Come on. Say you will."

Doing a banner is lots of work, he thought. And I'm busy with baseball. Will I have time to

spend on a banner? I like pitching. Maybe I should stick to that. "I don't think I want to do it," he said, not looking at her.

"Why, Alexander, you're the only one who can possibly win for us. Everybody wants you."

"No. And *everybody* doesn't want me."

"But you're the school's artist."

He wanted to say to her, yeah, and it was that honor that gave me that awful name Seemore, but he kept his head down and said nothing.

Finally Mrs. Cloud said, "You can choose your theme. You only have to use the number five in a creative way to celebrate the fifth anniversary of the festival."

Xander did not want to turn her down, and he *was* happiest when he worked with pencils and paint. But he was not sure he wanted to create a banner now. He looked up. "I don't know. Let me think about it."

All the way to the center, he had the feeling that he had let her down. She trusted him, and she always praised his work and made him feel good about himself and his drawings. Why couldn't he just say yes?

The center was crowded and Jeff was waiting for him. "I thought you weren't coming. You're late."

"I had to stay after school."

"You in trouble? You look like it."

"Naw. No trouble. The art teacher wants me to do something for her, and I don't wanna do it." He told Jeff about the banner.

"I thought you like to draw."

"I do." He explained about winning the best school artist contest and how he was taunted after that.

"You let something like that keep you from doing what you're good at and like doing?"

Suddenly he said, "But it's my daddy..." He stopped, sat down, and lowered his head.

"What is it, Xander?" Jeff waited.

Xander sat, with his head still down. Finally he said, "My daddy thinks I like to do nothing but draw. That I need to learn something I can make a living at or will get me a college scholarship."

"Aw, Xander, he didn't mean he didn't want you to draw at all. He just doesn't want you to spend *all* of your time drawing. He wants you to do lots of things." Jeff opened his arms and said, "To develop, man. That's what he wants."

"That's what you say."

"I bet if you went home right now and told your parents what you were asked to do, they'd be as happy about it as I am. But first, do *you* want to do it?"

"Well, yeah. Aw, I don't know."

"Where's your confidence, man?"

"Yeah, I'd like to do it."

"Then do it."

He walked home wondering how he would break the news to his family. He now knew he wanted to do it. But what would they say? Brandy would probably tease him and plant doubts in his mind.

At home he greeted his mama and went straight to his room. He lay on his bed. What if

I can't do a banner, he thought. What would I draw? Can I come up with a theme? Suddenly he felt it might be fun to try.

At dinner, Xander listened to Brandy with his mind on what he would say when it was his turn. His palms were wet and cold; his stomach felt weak. When it was his turn, he said, "The art teacher asked me to do our school banner for the City Spirit Art Festival."

"I hope you said yes," Mama said with enthusiasm.

Xander answered quickly, "No, I didn't. I told her I'd think about it."

"Do you think you can play on the team and do a banner, too?" Daddy asked.

"Sure he can," Mama said. "The banner won't take the whole season."

"Well, if you can do both, I think it will be wonderful, son. A good experience."

Did his daddy really mean that? Xander's surprised pleasure quickly turned to doubt. Could he do both? He wanted to please Mrs. Cloud, and now he couldn't let his mama down. The silence was deep as they awaited his answer. He looked up at his daddy and said, "I can do both."

In his room he sat at his desk with a sharp pencil, drawing triangles and long rectangular shapes, his mind on the decision he had made. He was happy that he had decided to do the banner, but he was worried. Could he come up with a theme that would please Mrs. Cloud? And if he got a theme, could he make it come alive? He decided he wouldn't think about it anymore until he had talked to Mrs. Cloud.

The next morning Xander walked happily into Mrs. Cloud's room. Before she said good morning, she asked, "Did you decide? I hope you're bringing me good news."

"I'll do it."

"Good! Shall we shake on it?"

Xander extended his hand and smiled, knowing she was a real friend. "We'll have to talk," he said. "I'll need to do some thinking about a theme."

"You know, a theme is just an idea. You, the

artist, create symbols that bring that idea to life, and the way you bring that idea to life is art. It can be music, poetry, a banner, a quilt."

"City Spirit, figure five," Xander said.

"What do you see when you think about our city?"

"I see people. All kinds of people, especially the friendly ones."

"Friendly ones," Mrs. Cloud said.

Xander thought about her warm friendly handshake. "A handshake. Five fingers. Friendship. Five Fingers to Friendship!" he said. "I think that can be our theme."

"Hmm, a handshake. Do you know what that symbolizes?"

"Friendship. You shook my hand when we made an agreement, and when my daddy meets a friend, they shake hands to say hello."

"There's something else. Clasped hands mean equality of status. In our city, we all are, or should be, equal. Five Fingers to Friendship. Xander, that's wonderful! We can get started right away."

11

Baseball training began with jogging, batting practice, and with Xander learning to become better at pitching. Xander noticed that his body was obeying him. He could not jog as fast as the others, but he stayed on the track just as long. Each day after practice, Coach said, "You're looking good, Bingham. You've got lots of talent, and when you learn some techniques, you'll be awesome."

Xander learned quickly how to grasp the ball correctly. The fingering was easy, but the true fastball was hard for him. He practiced the motions day and night. And even when he was not throwing a ball, he went through the motions in his mind.

Now at dinner, he was so tired he could hardly wait to get to bed. His feet hurt and his arm and shoulder muscles ached. He had no energy for working on the banner.

As Xander left the dinner table, limping, Mama said, "I think you're trying to do too much."

"Aw, Mama, I'm fine."

"He's all right," Daddy said. "That hard work gets him to bed early."

Later that evening after Xander had taken his bath and was readying for bed, his daddy came into his room. "Mr. Sterling came into the store today. He says you're doing good and getting better."

"He said that? I don't know how good I am, but I know he's working me hard."

"How about a good rubdown, son?"

Xander lay on his bed for his daddy to rub cool alcohol on his sore muscles. He enjoyed having his feet exercised and soothed with powder. "Wow, that feels good."

"I know."

"Did Grandpa Bingham do this for you?"

"Nope, he wasn't too interested in sports. But sometimes he did come to see me play."

"I bet he thought you were supergood."

"I don't know. He never told me." Somewhat agitated, Daddy said in a voice hardly loud enough for Xander to hear, "I didn't see that much of him anyway." There was silence between them. Then in his confident voice, his daddy said, "So when is your first game?"

"In about two weeks. We play the Lynxes."

"The regional champs! That's a real challenge."

"You think I'll be ready? And good enough?"

"Sterling seems to think so."

"But I don't think I'm that good," Xander worried.

"You won't know until the game is over, so stop worrying and do your best. Good night, son, sleep tight."

Xander pitched the ball into the high grass. He threw another and another. He had no more balls and started to look for them. "Don't go in that grass," Craig said. "There're alligators out there."

"Alligators? Can't be, stupid. There's no water in that grass. I'm going." The grass was over Xander's head. He walked farther. Suddenly something leaped up and grabbed his arm. He didn't see what it was, but he knew it was an alligator. Oh, it hurt so bad! "Ow! Ow! Ouch!" he screamed.

"Xander, Xander, wake up!" Mama was shaking him.

"Get it off, get it off, get it off my arm," Xander shouted.

Brandy and Daddy rushed into the room. "He has a cramp, a charley horse," Mama said.

"Theresa, you and Brandy go back to bed; I'll take care of him," Daddy said.

Xander had never felt so much pain. He

stopped screaming, but he couldn't hold back the tears. Brandy left the room, but Mama stayed. Daddy rubbed the arm until Xander relaxed and the pain went away.

"I knew he was doing too much," Mama said. "Tomorrow, you'll not go out of this house. You're going to rest."

"Oh no, I'm all right. I have to go to school. I have to practice. I can't stay home," Xander cried.

"Okay, okay, go back to sleep, now, and we'll see what happens tomorrow," Daddy said.

"What had your arm?" his mama asked, laughing.

Xander's scalp tingled. He wouldn't look at her. He couldn't bring himself to tell what his dream was about. "I didn't see what it was."

His mama was firm. For two days he couldn't jump rope, walk on the wire, or practice baseball.

However, he worked on the banner. He drew lines trying to shape the hands and fingers. He struggled just to get them to look like hands. Why had he chosen hands? He always had trouble with hands. "I just can't seem to get them right, Mrs. Cloud," he said to her one day.

"Have you looked at hands? Really observed them?"

"I see them in my mind."

"You have to look at real hands. Study pictures of hands so you can become familiar with the way they look."

"But I don't want to copy. I want to draw them."

She laughed. "Alexander, the finest artists use models. They look at the things they draw and paint. You can do that, too."

"Really? I thought that was copying. And artists aren't supposed to copy."

"It's not copying. It is seeing something so well that you can help others see it, too, with a new feeling about it. Take some time and just look at hands."

After dinner that evening he said, "I bet

my hands are bigger than all of yours."

"No way!" Daddy said. "Here, I'll show you." Daddy put his hands out on the table. His fingers were slender, with short nails, and the skin around the joints was loose and wrinkled. Xander put his hand on top of his daddy's. Xander's fingers were longer, but his hand was not as wide.

"What's this with hands?" Brandy asked. "I'd be in bad shape if mine were as big as yours." She held up her hands and looked at them admiringly.

"Hey, measure mine," Mama said.

Xander took her hands in his and felt how small and soft they were. Her fingers were long and slender. He thought they were more beautiful than Brandy's.

Everywhere Xander went he looked at hands. At the barber shop he saw interesting ones. Old wrinkled hands that showed the signs of hard work; hands with crooked fingers and crusted nails. Small plump hands with short pink nails. At night before he went to bed, he looked at his own. Opened and closed. Inside and outside. He even tried to clasp them to get the feel of what a handshake was like.

He thought of the trouble he had with the tiger's paw and wondered if he would ever get the hands right before the deadline.

12

On the day of Xander's first game, his whole family was there. Many of his family's friends were there, too. Because Jeff had assisted in coaching Xander, Coach Sterling invited Jeff to sit in the dugout.

Coach explained the strategy. Craig, their seasoned pitcher, would start. Craig and the coach felt that he could pitch a winning game.

If he tired, then Xander would go in and relieve Craig. "You're a rookie, but I know what you can do."

In the seventh inning Xander relaxed, feeling that he would not be called. The Mustangs were one run ahead of the Lynxes. Craig was still on the mound.

The Lynxes still had a chance to win in this last inning of the game. A tie would mean extra innings, and the Lynxes played their best in overtime. The Mustangs had to get them out this inning without giving up a run. But Craig was slowing down, running out of steam.

Craig walked a man. "Bingham," Coach called. "Get ready." Xander went into the bull pen to warm up.

Then a high fly ball went deep into the right field. Steve caught the ball, for the first out. However the Lynx Craig had walked moved to second. The next batter hit an infield single, and the Lynxes now had men on first and third.

"Your turn, man," Coach said to Xander.

"I'm depending on you to get them out."

"You can win this one for us, Xander," Jeff said. "I know you can."

Walking to the mound, Xander felt his stomach flutter. There were cheers and calls for him. On the mound he wriggled his shoulders and then straightened up to his full height. As he warmed up, he heard someone shout, "Do it for me, Xander." He smiled, knowing it was his mama. He tossed to his catcher, and within seven pitches, Xander was ready.

He stood still, looking at the batter leaning over, his bat raised. The catcher signaled for a fastball. Xander took his time, raised his leg, and delivered.

"Strike!" yelled the umpire.

Xander stood still again, waiting for the next signal from the catcher. The runner on first raced to steal second. Xander threw the ball. Not in time. Now there was a man on second and one on third.

Xander fired off another fastball, below the knee. Ball one!

The catcher signaled for a curve. Xander responded. Ball two! A pain shot through his arm. He wriggled his shoulder up and down. "Come on, Xander," came from the stands.

He sent another fastball sizzling toward the plate. The batter swung and hit a line drive to center field. The ball shot right through the center fielder's glove. The man on third scored easily. The runner on second sped to third base and risked heading for home. A long throw from the field landed solidly in the catcher's mitt, but the umpire ruled "Safe!" The Lynxes had won.

Xander walked to the locker room feeling that he could do nothing right. Why did he ever think he could play this game? Even though nobody said anything, Xander felt the team blamed him for losing. When Jeff came up to him, he could hardly keep the tears from overflowing.

Jeff clasped his hand. "You were in great form, man, and did a fine job. Don't see this as a loss. This is a beginning. I looked at you on the mound and I thought about Satchel Paige.

Hang in there, and when you're called Suitcase, know you can rank with the best in the league."

When he joined his family, Xander saw the disappointment on his father's face, and, "Can't win them all, son," was all Daddy said. Mama put her arm around his waist. They walked to the car quietly together. Finally she said, "That was a close game. You pitched good. If you had been the starter, I think we would've won." Xander felt a little better.

As they settled in for the ride home, Brandy said, "Don't look so sad. It's only a game." There was silence. "Say something," Brandy shouted. Then she lowered her voice and said, "All right, if it'll make you feel better, I won't ever call you Suitcase again."

Xander thought about what Jeff had told him about Satchel Paige. He looked at Brandy and said with all the pride he could muster, "You know what? You can call me Suitcase or See-more any time you want. Won't bother me none." He settled back and let the warm wind bathe his face.

13

As the deadline for the banner came closer, Xander finished a handshake that pleased him and Mrs. Cloud. But he felt that the banner needed something else. Just hands were not enough. "What if we put some people in it?" he asked.

"In a big circle, maybe?" Mrs. Cloud responded.

Xander looked at the banner. It was four feet

long and two feet wide. "I don't think a circle will work. What about a big bold figure five? In the center of the space shaped like a backward *C* we can put the handshake. And we could put the people in the other part. What's that space called?"

"You mean the counter space. Will we have time to draw people? How many will you need to fill in that space?"

"About twenty-five in all, I guess."

"We don't have that much time left, Alexander."

"Hey! I got an idea. If I cut them out of tagboard, it won't take long to draw in features." Within a few minutes Xander had made boy and girl patterns. He worked mornings, at noon recesses, and at night cutting out people and painting them the colors of all the races. He painted colorful ethnic costumes on some. On one he put a black sombrero.

Finally when he had placed them within the heavy black outlines of the number five, he felt that he had a balanced banner. He looked at it carefully. Oh, no, he thought. What was missing? Suddenly he knew. Xander carefully printed FIVE FINGERS TO FRIENDSHIP in bold black letters at the bottom of the banner. Now he looked at it and knew it was finished.

He rushed to Mrs. Cloud and handed her the banner rolled neatly. "At last." He smiled.

Mrs. Cloud carefully but hurriedly unrolled the banner. "Ah! You're a genius, Alexander Bingham," she said, giving him a hug.

Surprised by the hug, Xander didn't know what to do with his hands. He stood stiffly, embarrassed but very pleased.

That evening at dinner, Xander picked at his food.

"Something's wrong; he ain't eating. You sick?" Brandy asked.

"Leave me alone. Naw. I ain't sick."

"Are you worried about the contest?" Mama asked. "If so, that's all right. I'd be nervous, too. But you've been working really hard."

"How is it coming along?" Daddy asked.

"It's finished."

"Already? Can we see it?" asked Daddy.

"I gave it to Mrs. Cloud."

"Oh," Daddy said. "You could've let us see it first."

Xander wanted to shout, Why didn't you ask before now? But instead, he said, "I'm sorry, I didn't think you were interested."

"It's okay. I'm sure I'll see it sometime. Go on eat, man, and don't be anxious about it. Worry when you know the worst. You don't know that yet. Always think you're gonna win until you know that you've lost."

Xander sat in his room. Maybe he should have shown the banner to his daddy. Why? he thought. He's never talked to me like he talks to Brandy and other people. Is he pleased that I can walk the wire, pitch a ball, and make an idea come alive? No. He could care less.

He took out the drawing of the tiger. He'd had a hard time finding models for tiger paws. Most tigers were in grass that covered their paws. But he was lucky to have found a photograph of a tiger on a tree limb. Soon he had the paws the way he wanted them. He was so pleased with what he had done, he decided to give the picture to Mrs. Cloud.

The next morning he went to school early to present his gift. "Good morning, Alexander," she greeted him. "Did you bring something for me to see?"

"This is for you," he said smiling.

"How nice. Let's make a frame right now and put this up so everybody can enjoy it."

Xander made a cardboard frame and hung the picture on the wall. "How's that?" he asked.

"Perfect. Oh, Alexander, I'm so proud of you! There's no doubt in my mind that we'll win at the festival."

The days passed slowly for Xander. He went to the gym, to all his other classes, and to the center. He walked the steady tester and played games, but his mind was always on the contest. Why was it taking so long for the committee to let them know? Sometimes he had a burst of confidence and thought he might win. Other times he said to himself, With all the good artists in the schools in this town, how can I win?

Finally one day around two o'clock, the school clerk's voice came over the intercom: "Alexander Bingham, please come to the principal's office." Xander was startled. His heart thumped so hard and loud in his ears he was afraid everybody could hear it.

"Alexander," his teacher said. "You may be excused."

"Goody-goody Suitcase is in trouble," Ronnie said. Everybody laughed.

"Not See-more. He don't know how to get in trouble," said Steve.

Had he done something wrong? What could Mr. Moss want with him? When he turned the corner, he saw Brandy going into the office. Had something happened to his family? His knees felt weak, but he hurried down the hall. Mr. Moss's office door was closed but he could hear a murmur of voices.

The clerk was talking on the phone, but Xander was so worried he blurted out, "There was a call for me to come to the office."

"Oh, yes, Alexander, wait just a minute." A minute seemed like a long time to Xander. Finally she said, "Mr. Moss is expecting you. You can go on in."

"Congratulations!" Mr. Moss said as Xander opened the door. "We won first prize in the City Spirit Art Festival competition." Mama, Daddy, Brandy, Mrs. Cloud, and the vice-principal were all there.

"We're so proud of you," Mama said, giving him a hug around the waist.

"We're more than proud. We're overwhelmingly happy." Daddy stretched out his hand to Xander. When Xander clasped his hand, Daddy drew him into his arms and gave him a hug.

Xander took a deep breath. "Oh, man!" was all he could say.

Xander turned to Brandy, "They really liked it?"

"Obviously they liked it very much. Now don't let your head swell so big it goes bursting through that door. Think we can live with you after all this?"

"Yeah, if you say you're glad I won."

"I'm glad you won."

"We're all glad you won, Alexander," said Mrs. Cloud. "But I knew all along we would."

"Alexander, now that you know, we can announce it to the whole school," Mr. Moss said.

Xander felt light enough to float down the hall. My daddy hugged me! he thought. He thought about Jeff and what he had said about some people being unable to express all they feel. But Daddy was there for him!

He was back in his classroom, sliding into his seat, when the principal's voice came over the intercom: "Boys and girls, we have some good news. Evelyn Moore Middle School has won first place in the competition for the banner to be hung at the City Spirit Fifth Annual Art Festival. Alexander Bingham did the banner for us. Let's hear it for Alexander and for our school. We are all winners!"

Cheers rang up and down the hall, "Whoo, whoo, whoo!" Steve stood up in their room and said, "We knew he was a fine artist because he can see more."

"See-more! See-more! See-more!" rang out. Xander's scalp tingled, his chest lifted. He had done the banner and was a winner! Now he could have it all—play ball *and* draw! He spread his arms and clenched his fists as he exclaimed, "Yes!"

MILDRED PITTS WALTER is widely admired for her positive, realistic portraits of African-American family life. A former kindergarten teacher, she truly enjoys the company of children and relishes hearing what they have on their minds during her frequent school and library appearences. Their comments often surprise and delight her and always offer grist for the writer's mill.

When she isn't writing or speaking, Mrs. Walter loves to explore. She has traveled to western Africa, China, Cuba, Turkey, Europe, Russia, and all around the United States. Mrs. Walter has been honored with many awards during her long writing career, including the 1987 Coretta Scott King Award for Literature for *Justin and the Best Biscuits in the World* and the 1993 Christopher Award for Nonfiction for *Mississippi Challenge* (Bradbury). Mildred Pitts Walter lives in Denver. In 1996 she was inducted into the Colorado Women's Hall of Fame.